NOT YETI!

Alan Gibbons is a primary school teacher and started writing children's books in 1990. His central themes come from his own experience, and observation of children. Alan Gibbons lives in Liverpool with his wife and four children.

NOT YETI

Alan Gibbons

illustrated by Anthony Lewis

A Dolphin Paperback

To Year Two and all children, parents and staff at Prescot Country School, Merseyside

Published in paperback in 1995
by Orion Children's Books
a division of The Orion Publishing Group Ltd
Orion House
5 Upper St Martin's Lane
London WC2H 9EA

Reissued in 1998

First published in Great Britain in 1994
by Orion Children's Books

This edition published in 2006 for Index Books Limited

A catalogue record for this book is available from
the British Library

Typeset by Deltatype Ltd, Ellesmere Port, Cheshire
Printed in Great Britain by Clays Ltd, St Ives plc

Contents

ONE

Footprints in the Snow

There they were again, just like the night Mum and Dad disappeared, a trail of big, deep footprints in the snow.

'Same as the first time!' exclaimed Joe.

There was nobody to hear him, not here at the far end of the garden. Even Great Aunt Pellagra's ears weren't *that* sensitive, and they were like satellite dishes. Joe placed his wellington boot gingerly into the nearest footprint.

'Big,' he murmured, his breath clouding in

the frosty night air. No, not big, huge. Who-ever, *what*ever made these prints must be enor-mous. Joe followed the tracks. They led to Great Aunt Pellagra's garage.

It's in there, Joe thought to himself. Now, Joe was brave but he wasn't *that* brave. As he reached for the handle on the garage door he began to tremble, and not because of the chill December air. Biting his lower lip, he turned the handle slowly. The door creaked as it opened. Joe braced himself. He was ready.

'Jo-seph!' A brain-searing screech rent the air, stopping him in his tracks. Oh, not now.

'Jo-seph, where are you, you good-for-nothing boy?'

The good-for-nothing boy was hesitating at the garage door, wishing Pelly would leave him alone. Just for once.

'I'm here, Great Aunt Pellagra,' he answered.

'Get into the house this minute,' she snapped. 'It's way past bedtime for a boy of your age.'

Joe read his wrist-watch by the light from the kitchen window. Seven o'clock! He used to stay up until nine at home. With a heart as heavy as one of Aunt Pelly's puddings, he turned towards the gloomy house he'd taken to calling

Castle Doom. 'I'm coming.'

He could hear her muttering to herself: 'I didn't ask for that nosy neighbour to dump the little worm on me. Is it my fault my fool of a niece has gone missing? Boys, disgusting creatures!'

He followed his aunt through the back door of the house, and closed it behind him as quietly as he could. She hated noise. Having made only the slightest click with the door, he hung his coat on the peg and tucked his gloves into his coat pocket. Great Aunt Pellagra hated untidiness too. Concentrating as hard as he could, which for Joe meant sticking out his tongue as far as it would go, he began the third and hardest part of the entrance ritual. He stepped from the doormat on to the sheet of newspaper provided to keep the floor clean, and slipped off his wellington boots. Then he picked up the cloth which his aunt also provided, and carefully wiped the boots until they were spotlessly clean and quite, quite dry. Great Aunt Pellagra hated the dirt and the damp.

In fact, there wasn't much Great Aunt Pellagra didn't hate. She even hated Christmas. With just ten days to go, there wasn't a single decoration or card, not a tree, not even a sprig of holly. The only thing in the whole world Pelly seemed to like was her husband Herbert, and what a nasty creature he was. Joe grimaced; they were made for each other. He tried to sneak upstairs, but his aunt was waiting for him. He stared up at her. Great Aunt Pellagra was such a mouthful that he called her Pelly, but never to her face. He wouldn't dare.

As for Great Uncle Herbert, he was just plain Herb.

'Joseph,' said Pelly. 'I have something to say to you.'

Joe examined her face and shuddered. With her long, wrinkled neck, hooked nose, red-rimmed eyes and dark, loose clothes, she was like a great vulture, and he was her prey. 'Yes, Great Aunt,' he replied.

'We – your great uncle Herbert and I . . .'

Herb arrived right on cue. He was like an aardvark. This particular aardvark was squeezed into tight corduroy trousers and an even tighter peach-coloured shirt which bulged in between the buttons to reveal horrid Herb's pale, pink, blubbery skin and a belly-button the size of the Grand Canyon. Joe liked the idea of Herb as an

aardvark. He'd read about them in the encyclopaedia he always took to bed with him: *aardvark* – a plump little anteater whose name means earth pig.

'We think it is high time you earned your keep. You've been living off our charity for five days now. You can't sponge off us for ever, you know.'

'No, Great Aunt,' said Joe.

'There is,' she continued, 'nothing worse than idleness.'

'Nothing,' agreed Herb, his plump belly quivering like electrified blancmange.

'We've found you a part-time job,' said Pelly.

'Can you guess what it is?' smirked Herb.

'Unpaid galley slave,' Joe muttered under his breath.

'What was that?' squawked Pelly, her gruesome shadow looming over him.

'What? What?' echoed Herb, twitching his piggy little snout in annoyance.

'Nothing,' Joe replied. Sometimes he was a bit too daring for his own good.

'I should think it is nothing,' spat Pelly. 'Boys should be seen and not heard.' She was furious. 'Anyway, your great uncle has found the very job for you. You'll be delivering newspapers for his good friend Mr Murdoch. It won't do you any harm to get some work done before you go to school. We can't have you turning out like the lazy, good-for-nothing parents who abandoned you, can we?'

'No, Great Aunt,' said Joe, feeling his eyes stinging. He was dying to protest that his parents couldn't have abandoned him. They just wouldn't.

'But –'

'But what?' squawked Pelly.

'But what?' repeated Herb, delighted that Joe was getting himself into even more trouble.

Joe covered his tracks quickly: 'But you said I could do the round before school.'

'What's wrong with that?' enquired Pelly.

'Well, I haven't got a school,' Joe explained. 'The one I used to go to is back home in Liverpool, and that's miles away from here.'

Here was Grimsley, the most miserable little town Joe had ever come across. Sure, Liverpool had its bad bits, but this place was all bad bit. If the world had a runny nose its name would be Grimsley.

'Well, you've got a school now,' said Pelly. 'Your great uncle called in on Mr Mincebrains, the Head at Piranha Street Juniors. He's another dear friend of ours. You start tomorrow. Say thank you.'

'Thank you, Great Uncle,' said Joe in a dull voice. He could just imagine the sort of school they would pick. Skull and crossbones flying from the roof, children being fed to lions in the playground, in short just the sort of school you'd expect in Grimsley.

'Now, get to bed,' ordered Pelly.

Joe consulted his watch. The cartoons would just be starting.

'Can't I watch the cartoons first?' he asked. 'It's the Christmas show. Please.'

'Not educational,' interrupted Herb. 'Boys who watch too much television become nasty, idle and obstinate. They get square eyeballs and their ears close over. Besides, there's a documentary about the Great Javanese Slug I want to see.'

Joe sadly climbed the stairs to bed. When he

reached the landing, he allowed himself one final protest: 'You *would* like slugs. I wish I had some salt to put on *you*!'

'What was that, Joseph?' Pelly called up to him.

Joe's face drained of blood. She really did have ears like satellite dishes!

TWO

The Thing

Joe flung himself on to the bed and sobbed into his pillow, but not too loudly. If he was heard there would be trouble. He had cried the night he'd arrived at Castle Doom, and Herb had locked him in a wardrobe until he'd stopped. He still stank of mothballs!

Joe rolled on to his back and stared at the ceiling, letting the tears run in cold streams down his cheeks, but he didn't make another sound. Clenching his fists, he made a decision –

he would never let them see how miserable they were making him. He would never let them win. Never! He looked at the note propped against the alarm clock. It gave directions to the newsagent's.

Joe's mind filled with thoughts of Mum and Dad. He reached for the bedside cabinet and started to leaf through his photo album. It was a full moon, and by drawing the curtains back a little he filled the room with its gentle, silvery light.

'Please come for me,' he whispered, running his fingers over the first page. The photos had been taken the summer before by Mrs Pickles, their next-door neighbour and dearest friend. The pictures were quite good, considering who'd taken them. Mrs Pickles was very absent-minded, so absent-minded she hadn't even phoned the police when his parents had disappeared! And that's not all, she was even more short-sighted. When she was using a camera she sometimes missed her subject completely. Joe's family had a collection of photos of garage doors and empty lawns, of ears without heads and ends of noses. She hadn't missed this time though. The photos showed the whole

Kelly family on the Mersey ferry. Dad was resting his hand on Joe's shoulder, while Mum was giving his hand a gentle squeeze. Poor old Mrs Pickles had nearly fallen overboard taking it!

'It's not fair,' groaned Joe. 'I just want to go home.'

Turning the page, he saw the snaps of their holiday in Scotland. He smiled as he recognized the one of him kicking a football along the banks of Loch Ness.

'Don't go too near the water,' Mum had warned. 'Or the monster will get you.'

'There's no such thing as monsters,' Joe had told her.

'Really?' his mum had answered. 'So what's that behind you?'

Joe shook his head. No such thing as monsters, indeed! That's why he was here, wasn't it? A monster had run off with Mum and Dad Kelly. Joe couldn't think of any other explanation. Sitting up on his bed, he peered into the night. It seemed to go on for ever, clear and dark and peppered with stars. He used to love the night sky, but not any more. It just made him feel even more lonely.

He turned the pages of the photo album until

he came to a picture of his parents at a street party. In the background you could just make out old man Lockjaw's house. It wasn't like the little terraced houses which surrounded it. It had once belonged to a sea captain, and was big and mysterious in its wild, rambling grounds. Joe shuddered. Lockjaw! Why did he keep bumping into such horrible people?

'Everything was fine until he moved in,' Joe hissed.

It was true. Until the day Lockjaw arrived in the neighbourhood it had been a perfectly ordinary street, and Joe had been a perfectly ordinary boy living there.

Unfortunately, he had kicked his perfectly ordinary football into Lockjaw's garden. Joe closed his eyes as he remembered how it all began. In a way it was Tommy Jones' fault. He'd moved as Joe took the penalty, and put him off. How his heart had sunk as the ball sailed over the fence. As Joe had crept up the path of the new neighbour's garden, he'd begun to tremble. He already knew there was something odd about Lockjaw. Mum was always complaining about him.

'Wildlife artist indeed!' she would fume, pointing to the sign on Lockjaw's gatepost.

'What sort of wildlife can you paint in Liverpool?'

Dad had said there were always the kids, but that was just his joke. Nobody had really been sure what Lockjaw was doing, but they did know something funny was going on. There had been all sorts of strange noises and comings and goings. And as for the things the neighbours had seen! Crates marked *crocodile* and *tiger*, *tarantula* and *cobra*. They'd been really worried when a massive container had arrived from the docks, guarded by a couple of real heavies. Dad had sworn that he'd heard roars and growls coming from inside the crates as they were unloaded.

'Those were the weirdest noises yet,' he'd said.

'Definitely odd,' Mum had added.

As Joe had edged forward in pursuit of his football, he suddenly heard a terrible wailing and groaning, and it seemed to be coming from below the ground. Plucking up courage, he had taken a few steps further. As he reached the cellar window the wailing had risen to a heart-rending screech. That did it. Joe forgot all about the ball and fled for his life.

He was convinced Lockjaw was holding somebody prisoner, and goodness knows what he was doing to the poor wretch!

Am I to blame, Joe wondered, as the memories came flooding back. Was I right to tell Mum and Dad about the prisoner in Lockjaw's cellar? They'd gone to investigate straight away and that had been the last time he'd seen them. With a start, he remembered the footprints leading to Pelly's garage.

'What are you?' he murmured. 'Did Lockjaw send you?'

Suddenly he wasn't afraid any more; he was downright angry. 'You won't get me!' he exclaimed, his voice echoing loudly. Then he remembered the satellite-dish ears downstairs and fell silent.

If you're out there, thought Joe, brandishing a rolled-up copy of his favourite comic as a weapon, I'm ready for you.

He gripped the curtains and threw them open. There, staring back at him through the frosted window-pane was the strangest face he had ever seen. He only glimpsed it for a second, before he hurtled across the room in panic and, trembling violently, buried himself beneath a mound of bedclothes.

It was a snow-white face with a shiny black nose in the middle. It was covered with thick hair and a thick beard as pure white as the face

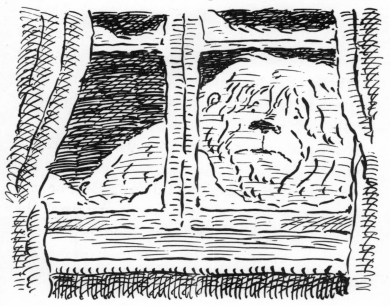

itself. What Joe remembered most vividly as he lay quivering under the bedclothes were the eyes. They were big and grey and as wild and sad as the winter gales. Joe lay there for hours, expecting at any moment to be snatched from his bed. He never was, and finally he fell into a deep sleep.

THREE
Followed

Joe's sleep was shattered at five twenty-one precisely by the ringing of the alarm clock. He flew out of bed as if pursued by demons, and pressed the off button to stop the din.

'Five twenty-one!' he hissed. He'd set it for five thirty and they'd wound it back to cheat him out of a whole nine minutes. Nine lovely, precious minutes were gone for ever. Why did Mrs Pickles have to send him to Pelly and Herb? Why hadn't she chosen another name out of

Mum's address book? Lots of families must have a Herb or a Pelly lurking somewhere, but why did *he* have to get stuck with them? As he stood barefoot in the freezing cold bedroom Joe shuddered without knowing why. Then he remembered the events of the night before. He looked around anxiously. What if it had got in? What if, even now, it was watching him, ready to pounce? Joe eased open the wardrobe door and glanced inside. Nothing. He peered under the bed. Nothing. Once he was sure that he was alone in the room, he braced himself for the final ordeal: stepping outside where the Thing was probably waiting.

He dressed, crept cautiously downstairs and hesitated by the back door. After what seemed like an age, he finally plucked up courage to turn the handle.

'Is there anybody there?' he whispered, peering outside. There was no reply.

It was nearly two miles to Murdoch's newsagent's. Two miles of holding his breath and glancing behind, expecting at every turn to see that eerie face. On one especially dark and windswept avenue he almost decided to go back. There *was* something worse than Herb and Pelly, after all. It would surely be better to return to Castle Doom and explain what he'd seen; but they'd never believe him. Joe didn't know what to do.

'Mum, Dad, where are you?' he said in a trembling voice. Then, wiping away his tears, he turned his anger on the Thing, wherever it was. 'Listen you,' he yelled as he ran on towards the newsagent's. 'You don't scare me.'

'Who are you talking to?' came a man's voice.

Joe jumped and looked round. In a shop doorway stood as thin and miserable an individual as he had ever seen. Joe opened his mouth, but nothing came out except a cloud of frosty breath.

'Cat got your tongue, boy?'

'No, I . . . I was looking for somewhere,' he stammered.

'Somewhere to rob, I'll bet,' the man grumbled as he went into his shop. 'Well, there's nothing here to steal.'

Joe stepped in from the cold, or rather he stepped out of one sort of cold into another. The man gave him an icy glare.

'Oh no,' said Joe. 'I don't steal. I'm looking for Murdoch's newsagent's.'

'You've found it,' came the reply. 'I'm Murdoch. So you're the new delivery boy, are you? You're late.'

Joe looked around the shop. Just the sort of place you'd expect in a dump like Grimsley. 'Sorry.' he muttered, grudgingly.

Murdoch heaved a huge pile of newspapers into a brown canvas shoulder-bag. 'You will be if you don't get these delivered. I hope you're not like the last young hooligan who worked for me. He threw my papers in the park lake, every last one of them.'

'How awful!' gasped Joe.

'Awful isn't the word for it,' snapped Murdoch. 'Criminal's what it was. They ought to bring back the stick for the likes of him. Six strokes of the cane is what they need. That's what I got and it never did me any harm.'

'No?'

'What?'

Joe winced. Why couldn't he keep his mouth shut? 'I said no. I was agreeing with you.'

'Hmm,' growled Murdoch, eyeing Joe suspiciously. 'Well, what are you hanging round here for? The addresses are all marked. Off you go.'

Joe sighed as he set off down the road,

staggering under the weight of the bag. He was all alone in a strange town and he didn't have a clue where any of these addresses were. Spotting a man walking his dog, he asked for number two, Dismal Close. Joe was half-way down the driveway when he heard a ferocious snarling. Two Alsatians burst through the bushes which bordered the drive, scattering clouds of powdery snow.

'Help!' Joe shrieked, as he turned tail and ran. The dogs were gaining. He could hear them panting closer and closer and closer still. He could feel their hot breath on the back of his neck. His parents would have known what to do if they'd been here. But they weren't. It was just Joe and two killer dogs. His chest was tight and his breath was coming in short, shallow gasps. It was no use. He'd had it.

He closed his eyes and waited for the worst. It didn't come. Instead, there was the sound of panic-stricken yelping.

'What the . . . ?'

Joe opened his eyes in time to see the dogs sail through the air above his head before bouncing across a frozen garden-pond. The moment they regained their footing, the Alsatians fled with their tails between their legs.

Joe examined the snowy ground. There, on the path, were giant footprints just like the ones in Pelly's garden.

'You saved me!' he said quietly. 'But where are you?' He was secretly hoping that *it* wouldn't hear. There was no reply, but he heard the tell-tale crunch of big, heavy feet on the snow. They were coming closer. Joe thought for a moment. Had it really saved him, or did it attack anything in its path? He didn't wait to find out. He was several streets away before he paused for breath. He leaned against a bus shelter, safe but more lost than ever.

'That's torn it,' he groaned. 'Now I'll never finish the round.'

Suddenly the snow crunched behind him. His heart turned over. He was about to run again when he saw a boy about his own age. He was cycling down the hill, whistling.

'Stop!' Joe cried, jumping in front of the bike. 'There's somebody following me.'

'Don't worry,' said the boy. 'He scarpered when he saw me coming. Big fellow, wasn't he?'

Joe nodded. That was an understatement.

'I don't think he'll come back,' the boy continued. 'Not if he's got any sense. Nobody tangles with cool Kenny Clarke, the Kamikaze Kid. Tell you what, why not jump on the crossbar? I'll help you finish your round.'

Joe stared at his papers. 'You're kidding!'

'Why?' asked the boy. 'I've just finished mine.'

'That would be brilliant,' said Joe gratefully.

31

'Are you sure you don't mind?'

'Of course not. We paper lads have got to stick together. I worked for a rotten newsagent once. He didn't pay me so I slung his papers in the lake.'

'Was that you?' gasped Joe. 'Mr Murdoch was going on about it when I arrived.'

'Oh, you're never working for that diabolical old skinflint, are you? You'd better tell your folks about Murdoch. He's a cheat and a swindler.'

Joe grimaced at the mention of his folks. He still didn't know if they were dead or alive.

'Anyway,' said the boy, 'let's get these papers delivered.'

'I'm really grateful,' said Joe. 'What was your name again?'

'Kenny. Some people call me Punchline.'

'Punchline?' said Joe. 'Why?'

'Because I tell great jokes, of course. What do you call an elephant with hiccups?'

'Dunno,' said Joe.

Kenny was already giggling. 'A woolly jumper.'

Joe frowned. 'But that doesn't make sense.'

'No,' said Kenny, his face clouding. 'It doesn't, come to think of it. I know, it's a mouse on holiday, isn't it?'

'I don't think so, somehow.'

'Don't worry,' said Kenny brightly. 'I'll get it right in a minute.'

Now Joe knew exactly why Kenny was called Punchline, but somehow he didn't have the heart to tell him.

'That didn't take too long, did it?' said Kenny, as he popped the last paper through the letter-box. 'I'm a real roadrunner, just like my dad.'

'Why?' asked Joe. 'What does he do?'

'He's a lorry driver,' explained Kenny. 'London to Leningrad, Blackpool to Budapest, Kirkby to . . . What starts with a K?'

'Kalamazoo,' suggested Joe. You see, he did spend a lot of time reading his encyclopaedia!

'That'll do,' said Kenny.

'And your mum?'

'She's a nurse.'

'Well,' said Joe. 'Thanks again for the help, Kenny.'

'Don't mention.' Kenny scribbled a note. 'This is where I live. Call round sometime. We'll have a laugh.'

Joe smiled. Not at your jokes, he thought.

'Who was that big guy anyway?' asked Kenny, as he pedalled away. 'He was built like King Kong.'

'I don't know,' said Joe.

But he did. It was the Thing.

FOUR

Piranha Street

Joe arrived back at Castle Doom with a smile on his face. The smile didn't last long. Pelly was waiting for him at the door, her heavy coat gathered round her like folded wings, her red eyes piercing the early morning mist.

'You,' she snorted indignantly, 'are late.'

'I can explain,' Joe began.

'There isn't time,' interrupted his aunt. 'We've got to go.'

'Go!' cried Joe. 'I haven't had any breakfast.'

'Then you should have got up earlier,' bawled Herb from the living room.

'Can't I even have some cereal?'

'No time,' repeated Pelly, seizing Joe's hand in a claw-like grip that made him wince. 'Now, off to school. I'll come with you this morning, but tonight you're on your own, so don't forget the way.'

Joe trudged wearily alongside his aunt, dreaming of food. A plate of toast dripping with melted butter, bowls of his favourite cereal, bacon and eggs with fried bread.

'We're here,' said his aunt at last.

Joe found himself looking at a large grey building. He had thought it was a derelict warehouse. As they approached it, Joe heard a familiar voice.

'Hi, Joe.' It was Kenny. He was standing on the street corner with half a dozen other children.

'Oh, hello,' Joe answered. 'Are you going in?'

'You've got to be kidding.' Kenny stared at the school the way a turkey looks at Christmas cards. 'I go to a school in Chuckleton. I'm just waiting for the bus.'

'Oh,' said Joe, disappointed. Somehow, he

had a feeling Chuckleton was a much nicer place than Grimsley.

'Anyway,' said Kenny, 'are you playing out tonight?'

'Playing?' cawed Pelly. 'Playing!' She glared at him. Kenny's eyes widened and his lips began to quiver.

Satisfied that she would hear no more nonsense, Pelly dragged Joe towards the school gates.

'Hey, Joe,' called Kenny, once Pelly was a safe distance away. 'What do you get if you cross a kangaroo and a sheep?'

'Easy,' said Joe. 'A woolly jumper.'

'Oh,' said Kenny glumly. 'You've heard it.'

'Kenny, *everyone*'s heard that one!'

'Then what do you call a ten-ton Rottweiler?'

'Sir,' Joe replied.

Kenny thought for a moment. 'Right again,' he said. 'I'll catch you out soon.'

'I doubt it,' said Joe.

'What are you laughing at?' demanded Pelly.

'Nothing, Great Aunt,' he answered, his smile vanishing at the sight of the hooked nose and the steely, bloodshot eyes.

Joe looked up at Piranha Street School. It didn't look the sort of place which would make you giggle. The ground-floor windows were covered with mesh, and there wasn't a bit of colour to be seen.

'In you go, then,' ordered Pelly. 'The Headmaster is expecting you.'

'Aren't you coming with me?' Joe asked.

'Certainly not,' she replied. 'You've got to learn to stand on your own two feet.'

Joe's own two feet led him to a door on the top floor marked *Mr Maurice Mincebrains*: *Headmaster*.

He knocked.

'Come!' came the voice.

'Name?' demanded a crusty little man scribbling away in a diary.

'Joe,' said Joe, looking around the walls of the Headmaster's room.

'Full name!'

'Kelly, I'm Joe Kelly.'

'Now listen, Kelly,' said Mr Mincebrains. 'Here at Piranha Street we learn the importance of work. Got that?'

'Yes.'

'Yes, Sir.'

'Yes, Sir.'

'Follow me. You're in Miss Hatchet's class.'

Joe hurried after Mr Mincebrains as he marched down the dingy corridors. His heart sank. His own school at home had been alive with the chatter of excited children. Piranha Street was about as lively as the cemetery at midnight. The Headmaster stopped abruptly at a classroom door. With a yelp of surprise Joe bumped into his back.

'Sorry,' he said.

'Sorry, *Sir*.'

'Sorry, *Sir*.'

'In.'

ABCDE

Joe entered the classroom and stood waiting to be introduced.

'Well?' demanded a thin, grey-haired woman. 'Don't just stand there gawping at me, you brainless little toad.'

Joe looked round, expecting to see Mr Mincebrains behind him. He had gone.

'Oh, I'm Joe Kelly. I'm the new boy.'

'Sit down, then, sit down.'

Joe found a chair and sat down. No wonder his aunt liked the place. Smiles were rarer than snow in the desert. None of the other children looked at him. They were all staring ahead, while Miss Hatchet wrote on the blackboard. After a few moments, tiredness began to take its toll. Joe's head lolled, his eyelids drooped and within seconds he was resting his head on the desk, half-asleep.

'Right,' declared Miss Hatchet, turning to face the class. 'Write.'

As the children set obediently to work, there was a knock at the door.

'Yes,' barked Miss Hatchet.

'Please, Miss,' said the skinniest little boy Joe had ever seen. 'The PE cupboard's locked.'

'Very well,' the teacher snorted irritably. 'I'll come.'

She ran her eyes over the scribbling class. 'Harry Skinnit,' she bawled, jerking Joe out of his doze, 'Come out here, boy. You're class monitor until I come back.'

With that, she swept from the room. Joe was aware of his classmates' eyes turning in his direction. They looked really hostile, but he didn't care. His eyes were drooping again and

41

his mind was full of sausages. Soon he was fast asleep.

Not for long. 'She's coming!' cried Harry Skinnit.

'The new boy's still asleep,' said a tall girl gleefully. 'Miss Hatchet will eat him alive.'

'What?' murmured Joe, barely awake.

'Miss Hatchet,' the girl repeated. 'She'll eat you alive.'

Joe was suddenly aware of the other children jostling him and gloating.

'Boil you,' said one.

'Grill you,' said another.

'Skewer and fry you.'

'Roast you.'

'Toast you.'

Help! thought Joe, now fully awake. Help!

But it was too late for help. The moment Miss Hatchet walked in, his classmates scurried to snitch on him.

'He *what*?' shrieked Miss Hatchet.

FIVE

Not Yeti

'I'm sorry, Miss,' whimpered Joe, shrinking back before the advancing teacher.

The other children were nudging one another and grinning at Joe's discomfort.

'Sorry?' sneered Miss Hatchet. 'Oh, you'll be sorry all right. It's the cane for you, you revolting little maggot.'

The cane! Joe's dad had told him about the cane, but nobody got caned any more. This couldn't be happening.

'But I don't want to go,' Joe protested, clinging to the door.

'Well,' said Miss Hatchet, her face reddening as she struggled to loosen his desperate grip, 'you're coming and that's that.'

'Never!' yelled Joe.

'Well, help me, you worthless idiots,' panted Miss Hatchet. Every time she prised the fingers of one of Joe's hands from the door, he clung all the more tightly with the other.

The boys and girls sprang to her aid. Joe was amazed. What sort of children were they? The sort you got in Grimsley, that's what.

'Get off,' he squealed.

It was no use. There were too many of them. At long last he was dragged out of the classroom.

'Mr Mincebrains will sort you out,' announced Miss Hatchet triumphantly, dragging him along the corridor and up three flights of stairs to Mincebrain's office.

'He did *what*!' bellowed an outraged Mr Mincebrains when he heard what Joe had done.

'But I was tired,' Joe explained. 'I had to get up early for my paper round.'

'Do you good,' said Mr Mincebrains, reaching for his cane.

Joe watched in terror as Mr Mincebrains brandished the weapon.

'This will teach you not to sleep in my school,' said Mr Mincebrains.

Joe braced himself, but nothing happened. Slowly he opened one eye, and saw a look of utter horror on Miss Hatchet's face. Opening his other eye, Joe saw why. Mr Mincebrains was tugging at one end of his cane with all his might.

The other end was being gripped by a huge white paw.

'You!' gasped Joe.

Poking its massive hairy head through the Headmaster's window was the Thing. Where had it come from? Maybe it had climbed, maybe it could even fly! It was the first time Joe had seen it by daylight. He studied it for a few seconds. Why was it so familiar? Then the penny dropped. Of course, he'd seen it in his encyclo-paedia. 'Yeti!' he yelled. That was it: *Yeti – hairy man-ape from the Himalayan mountains.*

'Not Yeti,' replied the sad, furry face at the window. 'Abnormal Showman, I mean, Ab-dominal Glow-worm, I mean, Abysmal Ploughman, I mean . . .'

'You mean Abominable Snowman,' said Joe.

'That's the one,' agreed the Yeti. 'I just can't manage long words.'

'Let go of my cane!' shrieked Mr Mincebrains like a petulant infant.

Without further ado, the creature raised the cane like an angler casting for fish, and flicked it. What was a tiny flick for a Yeti, was a great launch for a man.

Joe's tormentor was suddenly sailing through

46

the air, out of the door and down the corridor. Miss Hatchet stared in amazement, and then promptly fainted.

'How did you do that?' Joe asked admiringly.

'Easy,' said the Yeti. 'Feel my muscles.'

'Wow!' cried Joe, squeezing the Yeti's huge arm.

'Do you think she's all right?' asked the Yeti, glancing across the floor at Miss Hatchet.

'I think so,' said Joe, astonished that the

creature should care about such a nasty old trout.

'What's that?' the Yeti asked, alerted by footfalls on the stairs.

Joe ran to the door. 'It's Mincebrains! He's bringing reinforcements!'

Joe froze. He didn't know what to do, but the Yeti did. Without a word, it seized Joe round the waist and pulled him through the window.

'Just a minute,' Joe cried, remembering something rather important. 'We're three floors up!'

SIX

Escape

Being three floors up might bother most people, but it's nothing to a fully-grown Yeti. It began to clamber down the sheer walls of the school like a trained mountaineer, but faster. So that was how the beast had reached the window! For a second Joe felt very safe snuggled against its shoulder and was enjoying listening to its good-natured grumbling. Then he remembered; this was the Thing that had parent-napped his mum and dad.

'Let go, you big bully,' he yelled, beating his fists against its hairy sides.

'Stop struggling,' panted the Yeti. 'You'll make me lose my . . .'

Joe lashed out, dislodging them both from the side of the building.

'. . . gri–iiiip!' shrieked the Yeti as it tumbled earthwards, still clutching Joe.

The unlikely pair landed in a flurry of snow. For a moment, two thick Yeti paws and two skinny boy's legs wriggled in the snowdrift, and then they were free.

'Where are they?' shouted Joe, swinging punches at the Yeti's enormous tummy. 'Where are my mum and dad?'

The great grey eyes widened. 'You don't think . . . ? You couldn't believe . . . ? Oh no, not me. I wouldn't hurt a living thing, not even a fly.'

As the Abominable Snowman tearfully pro-tested its innocence, there was a sudden uproar. Teachers came running into the playground armed with mops, brushes and metre rulers.

'It's Mr Mincebrains,' groaned Joe. 'Now what do I do?'

The Yeti decided for him. Swinging Joe on to

its furry shoulders, it charged with an incredible turn of speed out of the school gates and down the street. It was sure-footed on the icy ground, which is more than could be said for the teachers. They were slithering and sliding, tripping and tumbling like circus clowns. Joe wasn't sure whether to call for help or cheer in triumph at his escape from Piranha Street. In the end, he just kept quiet and clung to the Thing's thick, white fur.

The appearance of a three-metre-tall Yeti in the High Street caused utter mayhem.

'Mummy,' asked a little boy. 'What's white and as big as a tree?'

His mother smiled. 'I don't know, darling, what is white and as big as a tree?'

'I don't know either,' said the boy. 'But it's coming straight for us.'

The woman looked. Then she looked again. Then she screamed – loudly.

'It's a monkey,' cried a hamburger-seller, as the Yeti skidded by.

'That's no monkey,' said a lollipop lady. 'It's a –'

'Monster!' screamed an old woman, dropping her shopping all over the snowy pavement.

'Stop!' ordered a policeman, raising his hand. The Yeti didn't even pause. It dodged the policeman and headed for one of the big stores.

'Oi!' shouted the policeman. 'You can't go in there.'

'What's happening?' wailed the Yeti, discovering an unexpected obstacle.

'Haven't you seen revolving doors before?' asked Joe, ducking to avoid banging his head.

'No,' panted the Yeti. 'I'm getting dizzy.'

No wonder. The beast was spinning faster and faster as the revolving doors picked up speed.

'Oh–oh,' Joe said in a voice hushed by fear. 'Here we go.'

So there they went, hurtling across the shop like a remote-control fur coat. They landed in a heap in front of Santa's Grotto.

'Stop that monster!' cried the policeman.

'In here,' ordered Joe. 'Quick.'

'Hey,' one man protested. 'Wait your turn. There is a queue, you know.'

But pursued Yetis don't queue. The Abominable Snowman thundered into the grotto, stumbled over a sack of presents, and landed heavily on Santa's lap.

'My,' said Santa, who'd been having a quick cup of tea, 'aren't you a big boy!'

It was only when he set down his cup that he saw just how big this particular boy was. 'Eek!' he screamed.

'This way,' said Joe, clambering back on to the Yeti's shoulders.

'Oh, not through there again,' groaned the Yeti as the revolving doors loomed.

'Just close your eyes and charge,' Joe advised.

So the Yeti charged out of the door, past a newly-arrived police car and through the crowds of astonished onlookers. None of their shouting and pointing had the slightest effect on the Yeti, but an abandoned skateboard did. The moment the unfortunate beast trod on the board, it panicked.

'Aargh-oo-aargh-aargh!' it screamed, sounding like Tarzan with his underpants on fire. It began to sway recklessly. The skateboard careered completely out of control into the road. Cars screeched to a halt, lorries swerved out of the Yeti's path.

'Balance,' Joe hissed. 'Stretch your arms out. You've got to ride it.'

'Can't,' yelped the Yeti. 'Never done it before. I'm scared as a snowflake.'

'Well stop being scared, you big wimp,' Joe snapped. 'Or we've both had it.'

The Yeti did its best to control the skate-board, but it was about as skilful as rice pudding on roller skates.

'Oh-oh,' murmured Joe.

'What?'

'That.'

'That' was a wooden ramp leading into a removal van, and there was no avoiding it. The wheel-borne Yeti shot up the ramp in a terrified white blur.

'Aagh!' screamed boy and Yeti. The Tarzan impressions were catching. Crash! went the roof of the van as they burst through it and, with a bump, landed on the road again.

'You went through that as if it was a paper bag,' gasped Joe.

The Yeti didn't reply; it was still shielding itself and its passenger with a pair of mighty paws.

'Put your arms down, will you?' pleaded Joe.

'How can you steer this thing if you aren't looking where you're going?'

'I daren't look,' blubbered the Yeti, which was looking more like a hairy jellyfish all the time. 'I won't look, I won't!'

'I give up,' said Joe. 'Half a ton of monster kidnapper, and you're trembling like a leaf!'

As they swept past a startled bus-driver, the Yeti shook its head behind its paws. 'I'm not a kidnapper and I'm not a monster.'

'Are you telling the truth?' asked Joe. He found himself wanting to believe the furry giant.

'Of course I am,' retorted the indignant Yeti from behind its paws. 'I'm as innocent as a lamb.'

'Big lamb,' snorted Joe. 'Oh no!'

'What!'

'Stop!'

The Yeti peeked between the fingers of its paws. 'I can't!' it bellowed. They were heading straight for a crash barrier, and behind it was an unfinished flyover. The road rose steeply before ending abruptly in mid-air high above the ground.

'Turn,' begged Joe. 'Just turn.'

'Don't know how.'

'Lean your body. Like this.'

Feeling Joe's body leaning, the Yeti followed suit. With a spray of sparks from the skate-board's wheels they skidded off the road and on to the neighbouring building site, finally plunging into a pile of snow-sprinkled sand.

'I'm alive,' the Yeti gasped in disbelief. 'Oh joy, I'm alive!'

'Thanks to me,' said Joe, shaking the sand out of his hair.

'Yes, thanks to you,' agreed the grateful Yeti, shaking Joe's hand with its giant paws.

'Forget the thanks,' grumbled Joe, easing his hand free. 'I want information. You said back there that you didn't take my parents. Well, if you didn't, who did?'

SEVEN
Lockjaw

'Lockjaw!' cried Joe. He knew the moment the Yeti spoke that it was telling the truth. He'd never liked the crazy newcomer. 'But why should he kidnap my parents?'

'They knew too much,' the Yeti answered.

'Too much about what?'

'Why, us of course, the Yetis.'

'Yetis? Don't you mean Yeti?'

'I know what I mean. There's me, my little son Yuet Ben and my husband Kambo.'

Joe nearly choked. 'You mean there's more than one of you?'

The Yeti nodded.

'But you said you weren't a Yeti,' said Joe, making a final protest.

'Ah,' said the Yeti. 'Lockjaw made us say that. He thought Edible Frying Pan . . .'

'Abominable Snowman!'

'He thought *that* sounded more exciting than Yeti, better for drawing the crowds.'

'OK,' said Joe impatiently. 'Tell me what happened. You'd better start from the very beginning.'

'Well,' said the Yeti. 'My name is Mabo. I was born on Mount Everest on –'

'Mount Everest?'

'Do you know it?' asked Mabo keenly.

'I've heard of it,' said Joe. 'I've got an encyclopaedia.'

'Does it hurt?' asked Mabo.

Joe thought about explaining that his encyclopaedia was a book, but somehow it didn't seem worth it. 'Never mind,' he said. 'Just carry on with your story.'

'Well,' Mabo began. 'We Yetis live so high up the mountains that we don't have much trouble with you humans. I'd only met one before Lockjaw came.'

'Who was that?'

'A lovely lady called Jane Tibbs. She was climbing the North Face when she fell and broke her leg. Well, we couldn't leave her to die, so we took her into our cave and nursed her. She's the one who taught us English. We were up to lesson fifteen when she got well enough to leave us.'

'Then what?'

'Jane went home and we saw nothing of human beings for a couple of years.'

'Until Lockjaw?'

'Until Lockjaw,' said Mabo, nodding. 'When Jane told people about being rescued by Yetis everybody thought she was mad.'

'Now, I wonder why!' said Joe.

'That wicked Arthur Lockjaw believed her, though. He'd just got back from Africa. The moment he heard about Jane's Yetis he organized a new expedition to the Himalayas. At first he said he just wanted to draw us, then . . .'

'He captured you?'

'Right again,' said Mabo. 'He put us in cages and shut us away. We rolled from side to side for

days. We were awfully sick.'

'You were on a ship,' explained Joe helpfully.

'If you say so,' said Mabo. She clearly didn't know what a ship was. 'Then Lockjaw locked us up in a dark, damp, smelly room.'

'The cellar!' exclaimed Joe. 'That must be Lockjaw's cellar. So you were the one who was crying!'

'Wouldn't you?' asked Mabo. 'It was horrible. We were so lonely and homesick. A Yeti without snow is like . . .'

'Fish without chips?' suggested Joe.

'Exactly,' agreed Mabo, who didn't know what fish or chips were.

'But why did you allow yourselves to be captured in the first place?' asked Joe. 'You're big enough. Why didn't you just eat him or something?'

'Eat him!' cried the Yeti. 'We're not monsters, you know. We live on mountain grasses. All Yetis are strict Rastafarians . . .'

'Don't you mean vegetarian?'

'Probably,' murmured Mabo. 'And we're just like you, but much nicer.'

'How do you work that out?' demanded Joe.

'Easy,' said Mabo. 'No Yeti would act like Lockjaw.'

Joe stared at Mabo. She was definitely winning him over. 'Anyway,' he said, 'what does Lockjaw want you for?'

'Oh, that's easy,' said Mabo. 'Lockjaw wants to keep us secret until he's ready to tell the world. He says we belong to him. He thinks we'll make him rich and famous.'

'You mean TV, newspapers, chat shows, that sort of thing?'

'All that and more,' agreed Mabo. 'Then you heard us calling for help.'

'You scared the living daylights out of me,' said Joe.

Mabo glared at the interruption.

'Sorry,' said Joe. 'Carry on.'

'Well, when you ran off we thought we'd never escape,' continued Mabo.

'Then Mum and Dad went to investigate.'

'That's right, and they were just letting us out when Lockjaw and his men discovered us. Only your dad and me got away.'

'You got away!' cried Joe. 'So where's Dad now?'

'We hadn't gone very far before Lockjaw and his men came after us in his truck. They nearly ran your father over. I tried to come to the rescue, but Lockjaw had a gun. Your dad had to give himself up.'

Joe stared at the snowy ground for a few moments. 'Hang on,' he said finally. 'How did you find me?'

'It wasn't easy,' replied Mabo. 'Do you know how many Kellys there are in Luvviepool?'

'You mean you went round the city asking for me?' gasped Joe.

'Of course,' said Mabo. 'How else could I find you?'

'But what did people say when they saw you?'

'They started talking funny. It sounded like *aagh*!'

Joe was about to explain when he thought better of it. He turned the news of his parents over in his mind. 'I knew they hadn't abandoned me,' he said.

'Anyway,' continued the Yeti. 'I talked to a nice old lady called Mrs Pickles. She was the first one who didn't say *aagh*!'

'That's because she's short-sighted,' Joe explained.

'I see,' said Mabo, who didn't. 'Well, she told me where you were. She said she'd sent you to stay with relatives when your parents didn't come home.'

'That's right,' said Joe. 'The worst relatives in

the world. Anyway, you've found me. Now what?'

Mabo looked quite crestfallen. 'Oh dear,' she moaned. 'I thought you might know what to do.'

'Me?' cried Joe.

EIGHT

Castle Doom

'Are you sure about this?'

'I'm sure.'

'Really and truly sure?'

'Absolutely positive,' said Joe firmly. 'Are all Yetis such cowards?'

'I am not a coward,' protested Mabo. 'I just don't want to get caught and sent back to Lockjaw.'

'Oh, won't they ever go to bed?' Joe wondered aloud.

'Why don't we just leave?' asked Mabo. 'We've been hiding here for hours. If we set off now we can be in Luvviepool by morning.'

'I'm not going until I've got my things,' insisted Joe. 'I can't go without my photos of Mum and Dad. That's all I've got left to remind me of them. Now shush.'

Mabo shushed obediently and the pair waited in silence.

'Look!' cried Joe triumphantly. 'Their light's gone off. Let's go.'

He rattled the handle of the kitchen door. 'It's locked.'

'That window isn't,' said Mabo.

'I can't get up there,' said Joe, eyeing his bedroom window.

'You can with my help,' said Mabo. 'I'm good at upbunking.'

'What?'

'Upbunking.' Mabo crouched and cupped her paws. 'You put your foot here and I give you an upbunk.'

'Oh,' said Joe, 'a bunk up.'

'No,' said Mabo. 'Upbunking is different. Ready?'

Ready or not, Joe couldn't think of anything

better so he put his foot in the Yeti's cupped paws.

'Hey,' hissed Joe as she lifted him. 'Not so fast.'

It was too late. Mabo swung him up with such force that he hurtled through the open window like a stone from a sling.

'Oops!' yelped the apologetic Yeti.

'Aagh!' cried the panic-stricken boy as he landed in a crumpled heap on the bed.

'Are you all right?' whispered Mabo as Joe limped downstairs and appeared at the kitchen window.

'Yes,' said Joe as he opened the door. 'I just hope we didn't wake them up.'

He let Mabo in and signalled for her to keep quiet. They held their breath and listened. There wasn't a sound.

'Right,' said Joe. 'I'll get my things then we're off. OK?'

Joe was making his way along the landing when he heard a door creak open.

'So you're back,' snarled Pelly.

'It's a wonder you dare,' growled Herb, 'after what you did.'

'I'm not back for long,' said Joe. 'I'm going home. I hate this horrible house.'

'Why, you cheeky young devil!' exclaimed Herb. 'I'll give you a thick ear.'

'You keep an eye on the little beast, Herbert,' ordered Pelly, as she stamped into the bedroom. 'I'll phone the police.'

'Police!' cried Joe. 'But I haven't done anything wrong.'

'Nothing wrong!' sneered Pelly. 'Mr Mince-brains told us what you and your accomplice did at school today.'

Herb was just raising his hand to strike Joe, when a look of utter terror spread across his revolting features. He found himself facing a fully-grown Yeti.

'Don't even think about it,' warned Mabo.

The beady little eyes of the aardvark met the big sad eyes of the Yeti. There was a moment's silence as Herb stood rooted to the spot, his jaw sagging.

'M-m-m-' stammered Herb.

'What are you gibbering about, Herbert?' demanded Pelly from the bedroom. 'Pull yourself together.'

'But it's a m-m-m-'

'I suppose I'll have to see for myself,' grumbled Pelly, emerging from the room. 'Now, wha- wha- wha-'

70

Mabo, obviously enjoying their discomfort, raised her huge paws and yelled: 'Boo!'

Well, that did it. 'MONSTER!' shrieked Pelly and Herb in unison.

As they slammed their bedroom door behind them, Mabo winked. 'I don't think they'll go bullying little boys again in a hurry.'

Joe smiled gratefully at the Yeti. 'I thought you wouldn't hurt a fly?'

'I wouldn't,' said Mabo. 'But in the case of those two, I would make an exception.'

Joe dashed into his room and began stuffing his belongings into his sports bag.

'Hurry,' hissed Mabo. 'I think I can hear something.'

She was right.

There was a phone on Pelly's bedside table and she'd spent the last couple of minutes telling the police that there was an intruder in the house.

'Galloping glaciers!' cried Mabo, as she stared out of the window and hopped excitedly from one paw to the other. 'It's a big gang of nee-naw men.'

'Stop where you are,' warned Pelly, as she ran from her room, brandishing a walking stick.

'Yes, stay exactly where you are,' ordered Herb from behind her back.

'Now what?' asked Joe.

'Anybody there?' came a voice from down-stairs.

'Up here,' cried Pelly. 'We've got them cornered.'

'What are you anyway?' asked Herb, examining the Yeti nervously.

'I,' replied Mabo proudly, 'am an Anti-social Stinkbomb . . .'

'That's Abominable Snowman,' said Joe.

Hearing the policemen on the stairs, Joe's revolting relatives half-turned to greet them.

'Upbunking?' whispered Mabo, seizing on the opportunity.

'Definitely,' agreed Joe.

Grabbing Herb and Pelly by the ankles, Mabo lifted them off the floor.

'Oo-waa!' they shrieked as they soared into the air.

'Now, madam,' said the policeman, 'where's this intruder of yours? Good grief!'

No wonder he was surprised. By the time he had climbed the stairs, the disgusting duo were dangling precariously from the banister rail.

And Joe and his furry friend? They were already out of the window and half-way down the outside wall.

NINE

Escape

'Hide!' yelled Joe as the police car roared after them, siren wailing. Mabo wasn't arguing. Flinging herself to the snow-covered ground, she covered her black nose with her paws. Joe stared in disbelief. 'You look just like a snow-drift,' he said admiringly.

'That's the idea,' said Mabo. 'Now, get down before they see you.'

Joe dived behind a hedge just as the car's headlights blazed through the night.

'Phew!' said Joe. 'That was close.'

'Too close,' declared Mabo. 'We need somewhere to hide. They'll be out looking for us.'

'But where?' asked Joe. 'I don't know anybody here.'

Mabo buried her great head in her paws. 'Oh calamity!' she wailed.

'Don't cry,' begged Joe. 'I'll think of something.' He stared into the deep, dark night, his mind racing.

'Well?' said Mabo hopefully.

Joe shook his head sadly. 'Nothing,' he said, shoving his hands deep into his pockets. As he watched the dejected Yeti wiping her tears, his fingers closed around a crumpled scrap of paper. Pulling it out of his pocket, he stared at it for a moment.

'Got it!' he exclaimed suddenly.

'What?'

'This.' He waved the tiny note.

'What is it?'

'I met this boy, Kenny. It's his address.'

'Will he help us?' asked Mabo.

'He'll have to,' Joe murmured. He was clutching at straws, but he didn't dare tell Mabo that. 'He's just got to.'

'Don't cry out,' said Joe, clapping a hand over Kenny's mouth. 'Promise?'

'Promise,' mumbled Kenny. 'But how did you get in?'

'Mabo gave me an upbunk,' explained Joe.

'Don't you mean bunk up?' asked Kenny.

'I know exactly what I mean,' Joe answered ruefully.

'Anyway,' said Kenny, 'who on earth is Mabo?'

'I am,' Mabo answered gruffly, sticking her head through the window.

'M-m-m-' Kenny began, his eyes widening in amazement.

'Shush,' hissed Joe.

'B-b-but it's a m-m-m-'

'Don't scream,' pleaded Joe. 'Please don't scream.'

'That thing,' gibbered Kenny. 'It's a m-m-m-'

'Stop him!' warned Mabo as Kenny's stammering got louder and louder. Before Kenny could yell *Monster!* Joe had clapped his hand back over Kenny's mouth.

'She's a friend, OK?' said Joe.

Kenny nodded and Joe took his hand away. 'But what is she? Some sort of overgrown teddy bear?'

'Bear!' exclaimed Mabo, as she clambered through the window. She looked quite disgusted.

Joe put his hand on Kenny's shoulder. 'Mabo's a Yeti,' he said. 'You've got to swear you won't tell anybody.'

'You can rely on me,' said Kenny.

Joe might have been able to count on Kenny, but he couldn't count on his dog. At that very moment a black and tan terrier shot into the bedroom yapping for all it was worth.

'Yikes!' squealed Mabo, starting in surprise

and almost tumbling backwards through the window.

'Stop him!' hissed Joe. 'He's scaring her.'

'Scaring her?' chuckled Kenny. 'What sort of monster is she?'

'She isn't a monster,' said Joe. 'I told you, she's a Yeti. Now, will you stop that stupid dog?'

'Down, Deefor,' Kenny ordered. 'Down, boy.'

'Deefor?' asked Joe. 'That's an odd name for a dog. Why Deefor?'

'D for dog, of course,' giggled Kenny. 'Haven't you got a sense of humour? Anyway, what's all this about?' he asked, restraining Deefor while Mabo shrank back from the tiny mutt.

Taking a deep breath, Joe explained.

'Is this for real?' Kenny demanded as he finished.

'Real as I am,' said Mabo.

Kenny eyed the Yeti warily. 'Fair enough, I'm convinced. What's your plan?'

'We haven't got one,' admitted Joe. 'We thought we might start at Lockjaw's place. That's where it all began.'

'Trouble is,' interrupted Mabo, 'the police are on our tail.' She'd begun to make friends with Deefor, gingerly stroking him.

'What we need,' Joe said pointedly, 'is transport.'

'And my dad,' Kenny continued, catching his drift, 'is a —'

'Lorry driver,' said Joe. 'Well, what do you think?'

'It depends where he's going in the morning,' Kenny replied. 'Hang on. He's got a book downstairs.'

Kenny left the room only to return a couple of minutes later with a big grin on his face. 'We're in luck,' he said. 'His first delivery isn't far from Liverpool.'

'Great,' said Joe. 'How far exactly?'

'Oh, about twenty miles,' said Kenny.

'Twenty miles!'

'Don't worry,' said Kenny with a wink. 'He'll take you. I've got him well trained.'

'Good job,' said Joe. 'Now who's sleeping where?'

Kenny sighed. 'I think Mabo's already decided.'

Joe glanced at the bed. Sure enough, half a ton of Yeti was snoring happily on Kenny's bed while Deefor snuggled happily against her.

TEN

Roadrunners

'Where's Mabo?' asked Joe, seeing the empty bed.

'Beats me,' replied Kenny, rubbing his eyes.

The boys wandered along the landing in search of the missing Yeti. As they passed the bathroom, their mouths fell open. Through the open door they could see Mabo standing pinned to the wall, and Kenny's dad wiping his face on her fur.

'This towel feels funny,' he grunted.

'He must have soap in his eyes,' whispered Kenny. 'I'll distract him before he sees her.' With an ear-splitting cry of '*Dad*!' he pounded downstairs.

'Kenny?' said his father, peering out of the door. 'And who are you?'

'Oh,' said Joe. 'I'm Joe Kelly. A friend of Kenny's.'

'I'm Errol,' said Kenny's dad. 'I didn't hear you come in.'

'No?' said Joe, at a loss for something to say.

'Anyway, what's up with our Kenny?' Errol wondered aloud as he followed his son downstairs.

Breathing a sigh of relief, Joe looked up at Mabo. 'What were you doing in there?'

'Just looking around,' said Mabo. 'He was there when I walked in. It's a good job he was washing his face.'

'Get in the bedroom,' ordered Joe. 'They're coming back.'

'I hear you need a lift, Joe,' said Errol, not noticing a blur of white fur vanishing into Kenny's room.

'Yes please,' Joe answered.

'To Liverpool?'

'Yes. That's where I'm from. I've been visiting my auntie, and I missed the train. I went back to her house but there was nobody in. That's why I came over to see Kenny.'

'Fair enough,' said Errol. 'You've got yourself a lift.'

Errol sat in the cab warming up the engine of the huge lorry. Joe read the brightly painted sign along the side: *Roadrunners*. Kenny stole a glance at his dad and eased open the back doors.

'Tell her to get in,' he hissed.

'Mabo,' called Joe. 'Come on.'

Mabo dashed from the house and climbed into the lorry. Just then Kenny's mum drew up in her car. She'd been working nights.

'Just in time,' whispered Kenny.

'Hop in, Ken,' called his mum. 'I'll drop you off at school before I go to bed.'

'See you, Joe,' said Kenny. 'Good luck.'

'Let's go, Joe,' shouted Errol.

'Oh Joe,' called Kenny from his mum's car.

'Yes?' asked Joe.

'If you have any problems just phone.'

'Thanks,' said Joe, clambering into the cab as the lorry began to pull out of the Close. 'I've still got your number.'

'What's in the back?' he asked Errol as they joined the motorway.

'Well,' said Errol. 'There's a load of cakes and ice-cream for a supermarket. It's mostly frozen stuff.'

'Frozen stuff!' exclaimed Joe. 'She'll . . .' He bit his tongue.

'I beg your pardon?' said Errol.

'Oh nothing,' murmured Joe.

Errol gave Joe a puzzled look. 'Anyway,' he continued, 'there's some fish and a few cases of whisky. That's about it.'

For the next twenty miles Joe sat with his fingers crossed. She'll be frozen stiffer than a lolly, he thought.

'Can you hear something?' asked Errol suddenly.

'No,' said Joe.

But he could. There was a loud bang followed by a low, throaty chuckle.

'What on earth was that?' asked Errol.

'Me,' said Joe hurriedly. 'I was singing.'

'Oh, I thought it came from the back.'

The chuckle was followed by a deafening roar.

'*Brrm*,' yelled Joe loudly, grasping an imaginary steering wheel.

Errol gave him a thin smile. He obviously thought Joe was completely nuts.

'Shut up, Mabo,' Joe pleaded under his breath. 'I can't keep this up.' He didn't need to. Everything had gone quiet.

As Joe directed Errol through the familiar streets of Liverpool, past its two cathedrals and the Pier Head, he felt excited. At last he had a chance to find his parents.

'Well,' Errol said as they rumbled along a main road, 'whereabouts do you live?'

'Over there,' Joe replied, wondering how he could get Mabo out. 'Drop me here. Hey, I've never seen in the back of a lorry. Can I have a look?'

'Sure,' said Errol. 'I'll open up.'

As Errol pulled the door handles, Joe racked his brains. How could he stop him noticing Mabo? 'Thief!' he yelled.

'What?'

'A man. He's getting in the cab.'

Errol was off like a shot.

'Mabo,' hissed Joe. 'Come on.'

The Yeti was staggering. It must be the cold, thought Joe. 'Are you all right?'

'Wonderful,' said Mabo, her grey eyes shining.

'I thought you'd be cold.'

'Cold?' chuckled Mabo. 'Don't be silly. Yetis love the cold.'

'Great,' said Joe. 'Get behind that wall – quick!'

Errol returned, scratching his head. 'I couldn't see anybody.'

'Oh,' said Joe, 'I must have been mistaken. Thanks for the lift. See you.'

'See you,' said Errol, wondering why Joe was acting so strangely.

ELEVEN

Presenting . . . Blister!

'So that's what all the noise was about,' said Joe. 'You're drunk!'

'Not at all,' protested Mabo. 'I only drank three bottles of whisky and I'm perfectly sober. Watch. I can walk in a straight line.'

Turning her back, the Yeti staggered unsteadily into the dustbins and fell over, making a tremendous din.

'Sober, eh?' said Joe, looking down at her.

'Well, maybe a bit squiffy,' Mabo admitted,

picking herself up.

'Just don't let me down,' Joe ordered. 'We've got to get Mum, Dad and your family out of there.'

Mabo peered over the fence into Lockjaw's garden and nodded.

'Hey,' said Joe. 'What's this?' Thundering towards them was a fleet of lorries. 'Mabo!' he said excitedly. 'It's the TV! Look: BBC, ITN, CNN, the lot. It's the big day; Lockjaw's showing off his Yetis. He's moving quickly!'

'He has to,' growled Mabo. 'I could spoil his little show.'

Joe nodded. 'Come on, there isn't a minute to lose.' With that, he started scrambling up the railings. 'Mabo,' he hissed, finding it too difficult. 'He's built a new fence. Give us a hand.'

As Joe placed his foot in Mabo's cupped paws, he noticed two very large men walking towards them. 'Oh-oh, I don't like the look of those two,' he said. 'Give me an upbunk before they see us.'

Mabo grinned. 'Here goes,' she said.

'Not too fast,' begged Joe. 'Hey, not too faaa-st!'

'Oops,' said Mabo as Joe flew over the fence.

'Oi!' shouted one of the men. 'Who's that?'

Mabo didn't stay to explain. Instead, she vaulted over the railings after Joe.

'Blimey!' exclaimed the second man. 'Did you see that, Blister!'

'It looked like that escaped Yeti,' gasped Blister. 'Come on, Thugsby, we'd better tell Mr Lockjaw.'

As Lockjaw's men headed for the gates, Mabo was pulling a furious Joe out of a nettle patch.

'Look what you've done, you overgrown hairbrush!' yelled Joe. 'I'm stung all over.'

'You ought to grow fur,' said Mabo. 'And it could have been worse. There's a compost heap over there.'

Joe glanced at the steaming mess and grimaced. 'Come on,' he said. 'Those men are going to warn Lockjaw.'

Boy and Yeti raced for the house.

'The door's locked,' groaned Joe. 'What do we do?'

Mabo shoved at the door with her shoulder. 'No use,' she said. 'He's got new doors too. This one's solid steel.'

'Hang on,' said Joe excitedly, 'that window's open. Give me a . . .'

'I know,' sighed Mabo. 'It's upbunking time.'

'Now, slowly does it,' Joe pleaded. 'Oh no-o-o!'

'Sorry,' mumbled a guilty Mabo. 'I don't know my own strength.'

A second later she heard a bolt sliding back and Joe appeared. 'Inside,' he whispered. 'Quick.'

Joe looked around. 'OK, where were you kept?'

'Down those stairs,' Mabo answered. 'In the cellar.'

Joe took the stairs three at a time. 'Whereabouts?'

'There,' replied Mabo.

'But this door's solid oak,' cried Joe. 'We'll never get in.'

'You're forgetting these,' said Mabo, flexing her muscles. 'Stand back.'

She took a deep breath and hurled herself at the door. Once, twice, three times she cannoned against it.

'It's no use,' said Joe.

Mabo snorted and charged once more. With a huge crash the door flew off its hinges.

'Look out!' she warned as she saw what lay

ahead of them. Her protective arm almost knocked the wind out of Joe's body.

'What is it?' he grumbled.

The answer to his question came in the shape of a motley collection of escaping creatures. Bats, wild cats, a shaggy bear, a scaly crocodile, a wolf, a hyena with a crooked smile.

'Anything else?' whispered Joe, as a few more creatures scurried by.

'That,' hissed Mabo, pointing to the ground.

Creeping past, not an inch from the toe of Joe's shoe, was a hairy tarantula.

'Ugh!' said Joe, shrinking back. He peered into the gloom of the cellar and saw a familiar figure. 'Dad? Dad, it's you!'

Joe threw his arms round his father.

'Don't I get a hug?' came a second voice.

'Mum!' Joe squealed, beside himself with joy. He hugged his mum then his dad, then his mum, then . . .

'Hey, calm down,' said his dad.

Joe nodded and released his father. That's when he remembered Mabo.

'Hang on,' Joe murmured, looking around. 'Where are the Yetis? Where's Mabo?'

'In there,' said his father, pointing to a side

room. 'We all had to share with Lockjaw's private zoo. It's a good job your mum and I like animals.'

Mabo was already inside, leaning over her husband and cub. 'What's Lockjaw done to them?' she cried. 'Why don't they wake up?'

'He gave them something to knock them out,' said Mum Kelly. 'Otherwise they'd have smashed their way out.'

'Just like Mabo smashed her way in,' added Dad Kelly.

'But how do we wake them up?' moaned Mabo.

'Water might do the trick,' suggested Mr Kelly. 'There's a hose-pipe over there.'

Mabo shot off and returned with the hose-pipe.

94

'Not full on!' yelled Mrs Kelly.

It was too late. A terrific stream of water hit the Yetis with bone-crunching force, hurling them against the wall.

'Turn it off,' shouted Joe. 'Mabo, for goodness' sake turn it off.'

'Are you all right, my darlings?' panted Mabo.

Her husband lay dripping on the floor. 'Mabo – it's you!'

The cub was next to wake up. 'Mummy!'

'Come on,' said Mrs Kelly. 'Let's leave them to their reunion.'

The Kellys climbed the stairs and peered through the filthy windows.

'What do we do now?' asked Joe.

'Hang on,' said Dad. 'I'm thinking.'

'Well?'

'I haven't thought yet.'

'What was that?' Mrs Kelly asked suddenly.

'What?'

'I thought I heard footsteps.'

They retraced their steps. The main door was swinging open.

'Oh-oh,' said Joe, dashing downstairs.

'What is it?' called his father.

Joe searched the cellar. 'It's the Yetis!' he shouted. 'They've gone. What if they've gone after Lockjaw?'

'We've got to stop them,' said his father. 'His men are armed. The Yetis don't stand a chance.'

Just then there were more footsteps outside the door. 'Quick,' said Joe's mum. 'Hide!'

The Kellys flattened themselves against the wall. In came Lockjaw's hired thugs, Blister and Thugsby.

'Crikey!' said Thugsby. 'They're gone.'

'Mr Lockjaw's not going to like it,' grumbled Blister.

'You tell him,' said Thugsby.

'Me!' bawled Blister. 'No way. You tell him.'

'No, you.'

'You do it.'

And off they ran, arguing furiously.

'They've gone,' said Mrs Kelly, peeping out. 'Come on, we've got to find those Yetis.'

'But where?' asked Joe, as the family emerged from the house.

'That looks a good bet,' his father answered.

At the end of a long path that led from the house a crowd was gathering in front of an open-air stage. They were eagerly training TV cameras on the closed curtains.

'Come on,' said Mr Kelly. 'Before they do something stupid. Kambo has a fit every time you mention Lockjaw's name.'

As they hurried forward, Arthur Lockjaw marched on to the stage wearing a broad smile. Blister and Thugsby could be seen arguing in the background.

'Ladies and gentlemen of the media,' Lockjaw began.

His men were hidden from view by the jostling crowd.

'You are here today to witness the first

appearance of the world's rarest creatures. I can hardly tell you the trials I have endured to bring to the public this astonishing discovery. May I present . . .' He tugged on a rope to open the curtains. '. . . Blister!'

Sure enough, standing before the TV crews wearing an embarrassed grin was Lockjaw's lackey.

TWELVE

On the Run

'Blister!' howled Lockjaw, beside himself with rage. 'What the devil are you doing there?'

'I was trying to tell you . . .' began Blister.

'Tell me what?' Lockjaw was a big man, and he looked even bigger when he was angry. His eyes blazed, his beard bristled and his bald head shone in the winter sunlight.

'It's the Yetis,' stammered Blister. 'They've escaped.'

'All of them?' roared Lockjaw, before

remembering the press clustering around him. 'Don't worry,' he told them, trying his best to sound in control. 'You'll see my discovery in a moment, *won't they, Blister*?'

Blister nodded unconvincingly.

'Hang on,' Lockjaw pleaded as the TV crews climbed back into their vans. 'Just give me five minutes. Please.'

The remaining television people weren't listening. Instead, they were staring at something on Lockjaw's collar. It was the large and very lively tarantula.

'What is it?' he asked, noticing their expressions.

Nobody answered. They'd also noticed in this order: one king cobra, one lumbering crocodile and one hungry-looking tiger, and they were all heading for the stage. Without further ado, the crowd turned and ran for their vehicles.

'You blithering idiot, Blister!' bellowed Lockjaw, still unaware of the growing menagerie around him. 'Can you imagine what your blundering has cost me? If you hadn't lost my Yetis I'd be worth millions . . .'

Suddenly he stopped ranting at the wretched Blister. Feeling the legs of the tarantula on his neck and the breath of the tiger on his arm, he began to wail helplessly. He stood terrified as Blister gingerly coaxed the spider into a net and Thugsby held the other animals at bay with a bamboo pole. Lockjaw's eyes narrowed as he stared past his henchman.

'What is it, boss?' asked Blister.

'That interfering fool Kelly,' hissed Lockjaw. 'That explains everything.'

Blister and Thugsby turned to see the Kelly family stealing away.

'I'll get you for this,' roared Lockjaw.

'I wouldn't count on it,' giggled Joe, watching with satisfaction as the animals closed in on Lockjaw and his men.

'This is our chance to escape,' came a gruff voice.

'Kambo,' said Mr Kelly. 'We thought you'd gone after Lockjaw.'

'We did,' said Kambo, 'but that lot beat us to it.'

He was pointing to the three villains surrounded by half a dozen hissing, snarling, growling animals.

'Joe,' cried Mabo happily, as the Yetis and the Kellys hurried away from the scene, 'Mummy and Daddy Kelly. We owe you everything. You saved us!' With that, the Yeti showed her gratitude by giving each of them a giant Yeti hug.

'Yes,' said Kambo, 'Without you we'd have been stuck in a cage for people to look at for the rest of our lives. Or worse, a lavatory.'

'That's laboratory,' said Mr Kelly. 'They do animal experiments in a laboratory.'

'Whatever,' said Kambo. Then he too reached out his mighty paws for a hug.

'Do you mind if we just shake hands?' asked Mr Kelly, rubbing his shoulder. 'A man can only take so many Yeti hugs.'

'I quite understand,' said Kambo. 'We don't know our own strength.' He sniffed the air.

'Free at last,' he sighed.

'I wouldn't go celebrating too soon,' warned Mrs Kelly. 'You're not safe yet. I mean, where are you going to live?'

Mabo's face fell. 'I never thought of that,' she groaned.

'I'm afraid you can't get to the Himalayas,' said Mr Kelly. 'We'll have to put on our thinking caps, but first, we'd better get out of here. I don't think those animals will hold them up long. Lockjaw's a wildlife expert, remember.'

'This way,' said his wife. 'I've got one of his vans round the corner.'

'Oh Mum,' said Joe, 'you didn't steal it?'

'Of course not,' she answered. 'I . . . borrowed it. Anyway, this is no time to quibble. Jump in.'

Squeezing all three Yetis in the back wasn't easy, but finally they were ready to go.

'I'm squashed,' moaned Yuet Ben. 'This van wasn't built for Abnoxious Snowdrops.'

'Abominable Snowmen,' said Joe. 'And stop complaining. It's not for long, is it, Dad?'

'That's the million dollar question,' Mr Kelly replied. 'It depends where we're going. Lockjaw knows where we live, so we can't go home.'

'How's about the police?' suggested Mrs Kelly. 'Or the RSPCA. After all, we've got the proof in the back.'

'OK,' said Mr Kelly. 'We'll see what the police have to say.'

'Were you really worried about us?' asked Mum as they roared down the road.

'Of course!' said Joe. 'And I hated Great Aunt Pellagra and Great Uncle Herbert.'

'Pellagra and Herbert!' said Mum, looking up horror-stricken. 'The dire duo, the poison pair; but what were you doing there?'

'Mrs Pickles didn't know what to do when you and Dad went missing, so she started phoning round the family. They were the first names in your book.'

'Oh, how awful!' cried Mum. 'I hated them when I was little. Was it terrible living with those two gruesome ogres?'

'Like being a cat in a dogs home,' said Joe.

'Poor Joe,' she said. 'Still, all's well that ends well. We're together and you'll never have to see them again.'

Which wasn't quite true, because at that very moment, driving straight towards them were not only Herb and Pelly, but a fleet of police cars. The first the Kellys knew about their arrival was when the leading police car skidded to a halt in front of them, lights flashing and siren wailing.

'What the devil!' exclaimed Mr Kelly, as at least a dozen policemen surrounded the van.

'That's Kelly,' bawled Pelly. 'I told you they'd come back here.'

'Joseph Kelly,' a voice boomed over a loud hailer. 'We know you're in there. Come out with your hands up.'

'This is crazy,' said Mr Kelly. 'Stay in the van while I sort it out.'

It was Mr Kelly who got sorted out. The moment he stepped out of the van, five burly policemen bundled him to the ground.

'Joseph Kelly,' said the officer-in-charge, 'I arrest you on charges of burglary, assault, and . . .'

'But he isn't Joseph Kelly,' cried Joe, leaping out of the van. 'I am.'

'You!' the policeman gasped. 'Is this true?' he asked Pelly.

She nodded. 'That's him, officer. Clap him in irons.'

'But he's a . . .'

'Right villain,' snarled Pelly.

'Dangerous criminal,' echoed Herb.

The policeman shook his head. 'I was going to say little boy. OK,' he announced to the police men and women. 'We're going back to the station.'

'Aren't you going to arrest the little horror?' yelled Herb.

'No,' said the policeman. 'But I might nick you for wasting police time.'

With that the police cars roared away leaving

Pelly screeching after them in fury. 'But what about the monster?'

'Would you believe it?' cried Mrs Kelly. 'That wicked old slug set the police on Joe.'

'Did you hear that, Herbert?' shrieked Pelly. 'She called me a slug. What have you got to say about that?'

'You're not a slug, dearest,' mumbled Herb.

'Is that all you can say?' bellowed Pelly.

'Yes,' said Herb, backing away.

'Herb,' Pelly barked threateningly.

'Yes, dearest,' he whimpered.

'Go and get them.'

'Yes, dearest.'

The aardvark was scared of the Yetis, he was even scared of the Kellys, but nothing scared him more than Pelly when she was angry.

'Jump in,' ordered Mrs Kelly. 'We're going, and there's nothing you can do to stop us.'

'Stop them,' shrieked Pelly.

Herb began to rattle the door handles.

'They're opening the doors,' yelled Joe.

'Go, go, go!' yelled Mabo. 'Step on the air!'

'Gas,' said Mrs Kelly. She didn't need telling twice. She accelerated so hard the van wheels began to spin, burning rubber.

'Herbert,' screeched Pelly. 'Stop them, you pathetic moron.'

Obediently, Herb clung to the door handle. The van wheels spun for a split-second longer then they began to move. The jerk sent Herb sprawling in a muddy puddle.

'Don't just lie there, man!' commanded Pelly. 'Do something.'

Herb raced after the van and clung to it grimly. A second later the van careered down the road, dragging him squealing along the tarmac. Not to be outdone, Pelly grabbed his trousers and was pulled along behind.

'Let go,' shouted Mabo as she stared down at Herb and Pelly, but they hung on for dear life. Something had to give, and sure enough something did. With a ripping sound, Herb's trousers came off in Pelly's hands.

'No-o-o-' cried Pelly as she parted company with her trouserless husband.

'Where did she go?' asked Joe, glancing over his shoulder.

'Straight through that thorn hedge,' said Kambo. 'Ooh, it looks painful.'

'Is Herb still with us?' asked Mr Kelly, glancing in the mirror. 'I can't see him.'

'If you mean the fat one, he is,' said Yuet Ben.

'Large as life,' said Mabo.

'And twice as ugly,' said Kambo.

'What do we do?' asked Mr Kelly.

'This,' said his wife, swinging the steering wheel. The van lurched, throwing the Yetis against the wall of the van.

'Help!' shrieked Yuet Ben.

'Oh calamity,' groaned Mabo. 'I think I'm going to be sick.'

'Be brave, my dears. Mrs Kelly knows what she's doing,' said Kambo. 'You do, don't you?' he added hopefully.

Mrs Kelly definitely did know what she was doing, because at that very moment Herb's fingers finally let go of the door handle.

With a loud '*Eeeek!*' the aardvark let go of the van and shot over a wall. The last thing he saw was a sign which read *Danger, Reservoir*.

'Help!' he screamed. 'Pellagra dearest, help me.'

But by then Pelly was half a mile away, painfully picking herself out of a thorn bush. Giving up any hope of a miraculous rescue, Herb closed his eyes. A second later he plunged into the icy waters of the reservoir.

'Is he OK?' asked Mrs Kelly anxiously.

'Yes,' said Mabo. 'There he is.'

'Well, fancy that,' said Joe, watching his former tormentor crawling on to the bank. 'I didn't know aardvarks could swim.'

THIRTEEN

'Going Our Way?'

'Why are we stopping?' asked Joe.

'Beats me,' said his father. 'What's wrong?'

Mrs Kelly shook her head as the van ground to a halt. 'I'll take a look.'

'Well?' asked Joe as his mother climbed back into the front seat.

'We're not going any further in this van, that's for certain,' she said sadly. 'This engine's well and truly finished.'

'Oh dear,' moaned Mabo. 'What are we going to do?'

Joe climbed down and stared along the deserted road. There was a road sign. 'Great,' he grumbled. 'Just when I think of somewhere for the Yetis to hide, we break down.'

'You thought of somewhere for us to hide?' asked Mabo excitedly. 'Where?'

Joe pointed at the sign. 'Scotland.'

'I don't want to go to Scotland!' wailed Yuet Ben. 'I want to go home.'

'I'm afraid you can't,' said Mr Kelly.

'But why not?' demanded Kambo.

'Can Yetis fly?' asked Joe, giving his dad a helping hand.

'No.'

'Swim a few thousand miles?'

'No.'

'Beam yourselves up?'

'I don't think so.' Kambo had never seen a space adventure, or a television for that matter.

'Then you're stuck.'

'Don't want to be stuck,' sulked Yuet Ben. 'Stuck stinks!'

Mabo scratched her furry head. 'Scotland, is it nice?'

'Nice?' exclaimed Joe. 'It's brilliant, it's got everything you need: lakes, mountains, wide open spaces. It's perfect.'

'Maybe it would be all right for a while,' said Kambo. 'At least until we thought of a way to get home.'

'There is one problem,' said Joe. 'How do we get there now the engine's blown up?'

'What's wrong with the way you got us to Luvviepool?' asked Mabo.

Joe stared at her for a moment. 'Of course, Errol's lorry! Mabo,' he said, planting a kiss on the Yeti's shiny black nose, 'you're brilliant. Why didn't I think of it?'

'Because,' said Mabo with a smile, 'you're only human.'

'Anybody need a lift?' came a familiar voice early next morning.

'What?' grunted Joe, rubbing the sleep from his eyes. 'Kenny! You made it. Is your dad with you?'

'Am I a genius?' demanded Kenny.

Joe frowned as if giving it a lot of thought.

'Hi, folks,' said Errol, peering at the huddle of Kellys in the van. 'I hear you need some help.'

'Did you tell him everything?' asked Joe.

'Not everything,' said Kenny.

'How much?'

'About that much,' admitted Kenny, making a tiny space between thumb and forefinger.

'So you didn't mention the Yetis?' asked Joe.

'Not in so many words,' said Kenny.

'Did you mention them at all?'

'Is this a trick question?'

'Kenny,' growled Joe. 'Did you tell your dad about the Yetis?'

'No.'

'So what are these Yetis?' asked Errol, examining the inside of the van curiously.

'Just Yetis,' said Joe.

'Abominable Snowmen,' explained Kenny.

'Is this one of your jokes?' asked Errol.

'It's no joke,' Mrs Kelly assured him.

'OK, where are the Yetis?' asked Errol, a grin spreading across his face.

'They're in that wood,' said Joe. 'They felt squashed in the back of the van so they went for a kip in the open air.'

'I see,' said Errol. 'So I got up at six o'clock on a Saturday morning to give a lift to a bunch of Himalayan monsters.'

'That's about it,' agreed Joe. 'But they're not monsters.'

'That's right,' said Mrs Kelly. 'They're vegetarians, and as gentle as kittens. Honestly, they're really cute.'

'Cute?' said Errol. 'Kenny, the next time one of your friends telephones for help, count me out.' He turned to Mr and Mrs Kelly. 'I'll give you folks a lift home,' he continued. 'But cut out this Yeti stuff. I'm a big boy now.'

'Not as big as him,' said Joe, pointing over Errol's shoulder.

Errol looked confused.

'Dad,' said Kenny, giving a low chuckle. 'What's white, hairy and the size of a house?'

'Oh, give over,' said Errol. 'I'm in no mood for one of your silly jokes.'

'Why not?' came a gruff voice. 'I like jokes.'

Errol spun round. 'M-m-m-'

'Don't say it, Dad,' warned Kenny. 'You'll offend him.'

Errol was staring up into Kambo's face in disbelief. 'But it's . . .'

117

'He,' Joe corrected, 'Kambo's a he, not an it.'

'Quite right,' agreed Mabo, emerging from the woods holding Yuet Ben by the paw.

'Am I dreaming?' asked Errol. He pinched himself. 'Ow! No, I'm not dreaming.'

'So where do you want to go?' asked Kenny, while his father continued to stare open-mouthed at the Yetis.

'Scotland,' Joe answered. 'Loch Ness. We went there on holiday last summer. It's a real wilderness up there. It'd be great for the Yetis.'

'Loch Ness?' said Errol. 'You haven't got anything else with you, have you?'

'Don't worry, Dad,' Kenny assured him. 'No more surprises.'

'Thank goodness for that,' said Errol, still keeping his distance from the furry trio.

'I don't think we'll all fit in the cab,' said Mr Kelly.

'Tell you what,' Errol suggested. 'People in the cab, Yetis in the back. How does that sound?'

'Wonderful,' said Mabo, winking at her family. 'Yetis like it in the back.'

'Fair enough,' said Errol. 'Off we go, then.'

Joe climbed into the cab, wondering why

Mabo had agreed so readily to stay in the back. The lorry was just turning on to the motorway when he had a thought.

'Errol,' he asked, 'are you still carrying that whisky?'

'That's right,' said Errol. 'Why?'

'Oh nothing,' said Joe, just as he heard the first drunken Yeti grunts behind him. 'Come on, let's find that wilderness.'

FOURTEEN

Nessie

They did find that wilderness, a wild glen beside a shimmering loch, but they weren't the only ones. Had they been less overjoyed at crossing the Scottish border, they might have noticed a zebra-striped Land Rover following them.

'There it is!' Joe exclaimed, his eyes shining with joy at the sight of Loch Ness.

The moment Errol stopped the lorry, Joe jumped out and ran to open up the back. 'Come and look, Mabo.'

'Come on, stir yourselves,' called Errol. 'We're here.'

The Yeti who climbed out of the lorry didn't look very enthusiastic. 'Not so loud,' she grumbled. 'I've got an overhang.'

'Hangover?' asked Errol. 'They've been at the whisky. You knew, didn't you, Joe?'

'Sorry.'

'Ah well, no harm done,' said Mr Kelly. 'This fresh Scottish air will soon clear your heads.'

'You'll be safe round here,' Joe added. 'There's everything you need.'

'It does look nice,' said Mabo, looking around. 'A bit flat, but nice.'

'You've done so much for us,' said Kambo. 'How can we ever repay you?'

'Just stay happy and free,' said Errol.

'That's right,' Kenny continued. 'It'd be dead boring without the likes of you around.'

'Yes,' added Joe. 'And the monster.'

'Monster?' gasped Mabo. 'What monster?'

'Why, the Loch Ness monster,' Joe replied.

Mabo stared at the gleaming ice which covered part of the lake. 'You mean there's a monster in there?'

'I don't like monsters,' whimpered Yuet Ben,

burying his face in his mother's fur. 'I'm scared of Lockjaws.'

'There isn't really a monster,' Mrs Kelly reassured them. 'It's just a fairy tale.'

'Hey, Joe,' called Kenny. 'Come over here. We can slide on the ice.'

'Don't you dare,' warned Errol. 'It could be dangerous.'

'But Dad . . .'

'But nothing,' interrupted his father. 'You could fall in and drown. Now come here.'

As Kenny grudgingly returned, Joe breathed in the frosty air. 'Isn't it great here?'

'Beautiful,' his mother answered. 'I hope you'll be happy, Mabo.'

'I'm sure we will be,' the Yeti answered with a smile.

'We'd better say our goodbyes now,' said Mr Kelly. 'It's a long drive home.'

Mabo took Joe's hands and gave a wide Yeti smile. 'Bye, Joe,' she said. 'Maybe you'll be up this way sometime.'

'You can count on it,' Joe answered, fighting back a tear. 'After all, we've still got to think of a way to get you home.'

With a last wave the Yetis set off along the

lakeside. Joe waved and turned towards the lorry. The smile suddenly vanished from his face.

'What's up, son?' asked Mrs Kelly.

Joe was staring at the road about a hundred metres behind the lorry.

'Isn't that one of Lockjaw's Land Rovers?'

'Crumbs!' roared Mr Kelly when he saw the vehicle. 'Joe's right.'

'Mabo, Kambo,' Kenny cried. 'They're here. Run!'

'You're too late,' came a loud sneering voice.

'Lockjaw!' Mr Kelly hissed. Lockjaw had sneaked unseen into the cab of the lorry. His men appeared, brandishing rifles.

'Watch them,' Lockjaw commanded. 'I'll get the animals.'

Blister trained his gun on Joe, Kenny, and their crestfallen parents while Thugsby drove his boss towards the fleeing Yetis.

'On to the ice!' shrieked Kenny. 'It's the only way.'

'No,' cried Joe. 'They're too heavy. They'll fall through.'

But the Yetis were already on the ice. Unable to drive after them, Thugsby and Lockjaw leapt from the lorry.

'Shoot the ice!' ordered Lockjaw. 'That'll bring them in. They mustn't get away. But don't injure them.'

As the first bullets hit the surface of the lake the ice began to crack.

'Back!' screamed Mabo. 'It's breaking.'

Freezing water gushed through the spreading cracks.

'Give up!' bellowed Lockjaw.

'Never,' retorted Mabo defiantly. 'You'll never put us on show like stuffed dummies.'

'Look,' thundered Lockjaw. 'Work for me or you'll drown right here.'

'We'd rather drown,' Kambo answered.

'Get off the ice,' ordered Lockjaw. 'I need you alive, you dumb furballs!'

'Won't,' yelled Yuet Ben defiantly.

'Leave them alone!' begged Joe, struggling desperately.

It was no use. With a terrible groan the ice opened up and the Yetis sank into the dark, chill waters.

'Oh no,' sobbed Mrs Kelly.

'You killed them, you monsters!' yelled Kenny.

Lockjaw turned to face them. 'I didn't,' he protested. 'It was their own fault.'

'It looks like it's over, boss,' said Blister.

But it wasn't. Behind him the water began to foam.

'What's that?' Joe gasped.

'Tricks won't do you any good,' laughed Lockjaw. 'I'm no fool, you know.'

Joe's eyes widened at the impossible vision before him. 'But it isn't a trick. Just look behind you.'

'He's telling the truth,' said Errol. 'Turn round for goodness' sake. Before it's too late.'

'Run!' yelled Kenny.

'Good try,' said Lockjaw. 'Aaagh!'

Why the scream? Well, at that very moment he'd felt fiery breath on the back of his neck, and spied scaly skin out of the corner of his eye. Joe stared in disbelief at the massive head, the gaping jaws, the endless rows of teeth.

'It can't be,' stammered Lockjaw. 'There's no such thing as monsters.'

He was wrong of course, and just to prove it, Nessie stretched her mighty neck. Lockjaw and his men cowered, their mouths gaping open.

'You *can't*,' they whined.

But she could. With a *glop* and a *yunk*, a *slurp* and a *burp*, they were gone.

'Do you think she'll eat us, Dad?' asked Kenny.

'Of course not,' came a familiar voice. 'I think she prefers the taste of baddies.'

'Mabo!' exclaimed Joe. 'Where are you?'

'Here,' said the Yeti, wading out of the frozen Loch, followed by Kambo and Yuet Ben.

'It's a good job we're used to the cold,' said Kambo shaking his fur, and soaking everybody in the process. Nessie watched the little group on the banks of the lake for a moment, then slid back into the icy waters.

'Well,' said Joe, 'it looks like you really are

free this time.'

'That's right,' said Kenny. 'Scotland's got its first Antarctic Crowbar.'

'You mean Ambidextrous Sandwich,' giggled Mrs Kelly.

'No,' chuckled Joe. 'You mean Antiseptic Sausage.'

The three Yetis took a deep breath and replied with a triumphant cry which echoed from glen to glen: 'That's Abominable Snowman!'